For Alexander and Lauren, with love —C.W.M.

For Taylor, Elisabeth, Caroline, and Turner, with love —M.W.

With sympathy to anyone who's ever moved —Boomer

ISBN 0-590-63487-9

Text copyright © 1994 by Constance W. McGeorge.
Illustrations copyright © 1994 by Mary Whyte.
All rights reserved. Published by Scholastic Inc.,
555 Broadway, New York, NY 10012,
by arrangement with Chronicle Books.

SCHOLASTIC and associated logos are trademarks and/or registered trademarks of Scholastic Inc.

12 11 10 9 8 7 6 5 4 3   8 9/9 0 1 2 3/0

Printed in the U.S.A.   08

First Scholastic printing, January 1997

Boomer's Big Day

By Constance W. McGeorge
Illustrated by Mary Whyte

SCHOLASTIC INC.
New York Toronto London Auckland Sydney

It was just after breakfast, and Boomer
was waiting to be taken for his daily walk
around the neighborhood.

But Boomer soon discovered this was not going to be an ordinary day. No one left the house after breakfast. No one would stop what they were doing to play with him. Everyone was very, very busy.

Boomer decided it was going to be one of those days when he had to play all by himself.

He searched the house for his favorite toy, an old green tennis ball. He looked in his toy basket—no ball. He looked under the sofa—no ball. He looked under all the beds in the house. But his ball was nowhere to be found.

Suddenly, the doorbell rang. Boomer barked and barked, but everyone told him to be quiet. Then strangers carrying large boxes came through the front door and into the house.

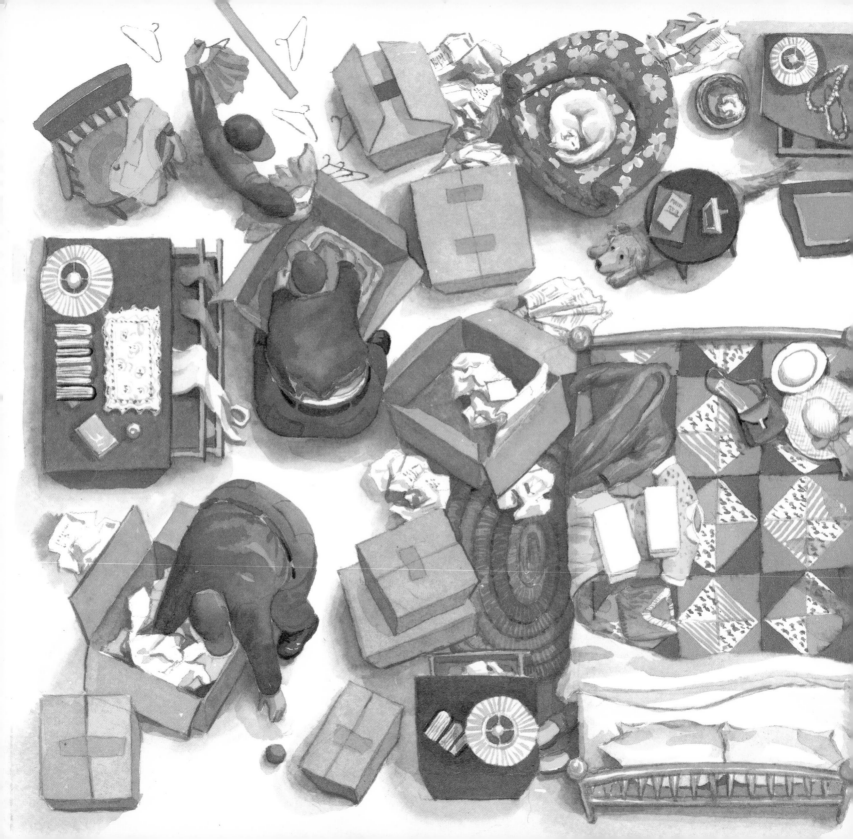

Soon there was activity everywhere. Boxes appeared in every room of the house. The strangers started pulling things out of closets, out of drawers, and out of cupboards.

Then they packed everything into boxes, and one by one, the boxes were carried out of the house.

Before Boomer knew it, the house was empty.

While the strangers loaded the boxes and furniture into a large truck parked in front of the house, Boomer's family loaded its van.

Finally, Boomer was led out of the house. He was told he was going for a ride. But lots of other things seemed to be going for a ride, too.

Boomer was very confused.

The ride was unlike any other Boomer had
ever taken. He could hardly see out the window.
Packages kept falling on him. The ride lasted a
very long time.

Finally, the van stopped in front of a house Boomer had never seen before. There were strange trees, strange flowers, and strange people passing by.

Boomer wondered where he was.

Boomer walked cautiously up to the front door of the house. He peeked in. The house was empty.

While the strangers unloaded the truck, and his family unloaded its van, Boomer went inside. He wandered from room to room. There was nothing to do and no one to play with.

Then Boomer discovered the backyard.

He couldn't believe his eyes!
There were things to sniff . . .

holes to dig . . .

squirrels to chase . . .

and best of all . . . there were new friends to be made!

At the end of the day, Boomer went inside. Instead of being empty, the house was now full of furniture and boxes.

Boomer found his dinner bowl in the kitchen. His bed had been unpacked, too. And there, beside it, was his old green tennis ball.

Boomer wagged his tail. Then, happy to be home, he curled up and went to sleep.